A RHYMING DICTIONARY

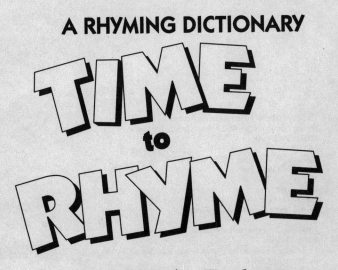

TIME to RHYME

by Marvin Terban

illustrated by Chris L. Demarest

Wordsong
Boyds Mills Press

Text copyright © 1994 by Marvin Terban
Illustrations copyright © 1994 by Chris L. Demarest

Published by Wordsong
Boyds Mills Press, Inc.
A Highlights Company
815 Church Street
Honesdale, Pennsylvania 18431
Printed in the United States of America

Publisher Cataloging-in-Publication Data
Terban, Marvin.
    Time to rhyme : a rhyming dictionary / by Marvin Terban ;
illustrated by Chris L. Demarest.—1st ed.
[96]p. : ill. ; cm.
Includes index.
Summary : This title includes a list of words that rhyme, which will help
children to write poems, and examples of poems.
Hardcover ISBN 1-56397-128-3 Paperback ISBN 1-56397-630-7
1. Poetry—Dictionaries. 2. Children's poetry. [1. Poetry.]
I. Demarest, Chris L., ill. II. Title.
808.1—dc20   1994   CIP
Library of Congress Catalog Card Number 93-60242

First Boyds Mills Press paperback edition, 1996
Book designed by Tim Gillner
The text of this book is set in 13-point Galliard.
The illustrations are done in pen and ink.
Reinforced trade edition

10 9 8 7 6 5 4

Reprinted by arrangement with Boyds Mills Press.

Table of Contents

• •

• •

About Rhymes and This Book

What Are Rhymes?

Rhymes are words that sound alike at the end. Say "sing," "ring," and "wing." They all have different sounds at the beginning, but they all have the same sound at the end. They rhyme.

Why Use Rhymes?

Rhymes are musical words. They make language sing. Rhymes can add fun and zip to whatever you write. Rhymes can sometimes make things easier to remember, too.

What Rhymes?

Poems sometimes rhyme:

> *One, two,*
> *Buckle my shoe;*
>
> *Three, four,*
> *Shut the door;*
>
> *Five, six,*
> *Pick up sticks;*
>
> *Seven, eight,*
> *Lay them straight;*
>
> *Nine, ten,*
> *A big fat hen.*
>
> —Mother Goose

Songs often rhyme:

> *Hush, little baby, don't say a word,*
> *Papa's gonna buy you a mockingbird.*
> *If that mockingbird won't sing,*
> *Papa's gonna buy you a diamond ring.*
> *If that diamond ring turns brass,*
> *Papa's gonna buy you a looking glass.*
>
> —American Folk Song

Greeting cards usually rhyme. They can be serious or funny:

> *This card is sent to you, my dear,*
> *Because I heard you're sick;*
> *I send you love and lots of cheer,*
> *And hope you're better quick.*

> *Happy birthday to you.*
> *You belong in a zoo.*
> *You look like a monkey,*
> *And you act like one, too.*

Signs, posters, slogans, and **sayings** are sometimes written in rhyme to help get the messages across with more spark and snap. Rhymes also make them fun to say and easier to remember:

> *At two today,*
> *Come see our play.*
> *You'll like what you see,*
> *And the tickets are free!*

VOTE FOR KATE.
SHE IS GREAT!

> *The fair starts at eight,*
> *So don't be late.*
> *We hate to wait!*

> *Early to bed and early to rise,*
> *Makes a man healthy, wealthy, and wise.*
> —Benjamin Franklin

How to Use This Book

Think of a word you want to find rhymes for.

Look up that word in the alphabetical list that begins on page 44.

After the word, you will find a page number and a group number. Turn to the page and find that group, and you will see the words that rhyme with your word.

That's all there is to it!

Some Things to Watch Out For

Not all words that rhyme have exactly the same spelling at the end. The following words all rhyme, but notice how differently the same rhyming sound is spelled:

bird, heard, herd, purred, stirred, word

To make it easy for you to find the rhyming words you need, all the words that rhyme are grouped together no matter how they are spelled.

Let's Try It Out

Suppose you want to make up a song or cheer about your school, and you want it to rhyme. Look up "school" in the alphabetical list. You'll find the words that rhyme with **"school"** on page 33, group 159 ("cool, drool, pool, rule, tool," etc.).

Now think of words that have to do with school and look them up, too:
    read, feed, need, speed, etc. (page 22, group 66)
    write, bright, might, right, etc. (page 30, group 128)
    learn, burn, earn, turn, etc. (page 41, group 227)
    teach, each, reach, speech, etc. (page 20, group 52)

fun, run, sun, won, etc. (page 39, group 214)
play, day, stay, they, etc. (page 19, group 50)
friends, bends, ends, lends, etc. (page 23, group 77)
sports, courts, forts, warts, etc. (page 34, group 175)

By the way, you won't find **"friends"** and **"sports"** on the alphabetical list. But you will find **"friend"** and **"sport."** Just add **"s"** to the words that rhyme with those words.

Play around with all the rhyming words you find. Keep trying different rhyming lines. Remember that the lines you write have to make sense as well as rhyme. Sometimes you won't be able to make up good rhyming lines that make sense. Think of other words. Try finding rhymes for them. Make up new lines. You'll like some of the lines and you'll cross out others. After many tries, you'll have a finished poem, song, cheer, or rap.

We learn all day
And then we play.

On the fields and on the courts,
We are always tops in sports.

We write and write
With all our might.
What we write
Is really bright.

Here we learn
All we need,
How to write
And how to read.

Does Every Line in a Row Have to Rhyme?

When you are writing your poem or song, not every line in a row has to rhyme with the same sound. Here's a famous song in which the ends of lines 1 and 2 rhyme with each other ("thee" and "liberty"). Lines 4, 5, and 6 rhyme with another sound ("died," "pride," and "mountainside"). Lines 3 and 7 rhyme with still another sound ("sing" and "ring").

> *My country 'tis of thee,*
> *Sweet land of liberty,*
> *Of thee I sing.*
> *Land where my fathers died,*
> *Land of the Pilgrims' pride,*
> *From every mountainside,*
> *Let freedom ring.*
>   —Samuel Francis Smith

You could write a song or poem that rhymes like the one above. You can make every other line rhyme with the same sound. Or, the first two lines could rhyme with one sound, and the next two lines could rhyme with another sound. There are lots of possibilities. Whatever sounds good to you is fine.

A Word about Vocabulary

You'll probably know what most of the words in this book mean, but there may be a few you have to look up in the dictionary, like "sphere" or "tweed" or "crave." When you learn what a new word means, you might find that it's just the word you were looking for.

What's Not in This Book

The English language has hundreds of thousands of words. Most of them are not in this book. Only common one-syllable words are in this book. If you can think of longer words that rhyme and make sense, definitely use them.

After you've gotten used to this first rhyming dictionary, you will be able to use a bigger rhyming dictionary that contains longer words and a harder vocabulary. For now, for you, the beginning author, poet, songwriter, or slogan maker, this book should be perfect.

Now it's time to rhyme.

• •

> What does the picture on the cover mean? See page 15, group 12, and you'll know.

Groups of Rhyming Words

1
ah, baa, bah, blah, ha, ma, pa

2
blab, cab, crab, dab, drab, gab, grab, jab, nab, scab, slab, stab, tab

3
ace, base, bass, brace, case, chase, face, grace, lace, pace, place, race, space, trace, vase

4
back, black, crack, jack, knack, lack, pack, quack, rack, sack, shack, smack, snack, stack, tack, track, whack

5
act, backed, cracked, fact, jacked, lacked, packed, pact, quacked, smacked, snacked, stacked, tacked, tact, tracked, whacked

6
ad, add, bad, dad, fad, glad, had, lad, mad, pad, plaid, sad

7
aid, blade, braid, fade, glade, grade, laid, made, maid, paid, prayed, preyed, raid, shade, spade, sprayed, stayed, strayed, swayed, they'd, trade, wade, weighed

Jack has a cracker snack,
While sitting in his shady shack.
He packs his snack up in his sack,
And wears it to the shack and back.

8
calf, graph, half, laugh, staff

9
craft, draft, laughed, raft

10
bag, brag, drag, flag, gag, hag, nag, rag, sag, shag, snag, stag, tag, wag

11
age, cage, gauge, page, rage, sage, stage, wage

12
ail, ale, bail, bale, braille, fail, frail, gale, grail, hail, hale, jail, mail, male, nail, pail, pale, quail, rail, sail, sale, scale, snail, stale, tail, tale, they'll, trail, veil, wail, whale

● ● ● ● ● ● ● ● ● ● ● ● ● ●

Can't afford a plane to Spain?
Why not take a train to Maine!

● ● ● ● ● ● ● ● ● ● ● ● ● ●

13
brain, cane, chain, crane, drain, gain, grain, lane, main, Maine, mane, pain, pane, plain, plane, rain, reign, rein, sane, Spain, sprain, stain, strain, train, vain, vane, vein

14
faint, paint, quaint, saint

15
ache, bake, brake, break, cake, drake, fake, flake, lake, make, rake, shake, snake, stake, steak, take, wake

● ● ● ● ● ● ● ● ● ● ● ● ● ● ●

Never bake a snake in a cake,
Unless the snake you bake is
fake.

● ● ● ● ● ● ● ● ● ● ● ● ● ●

I knew a boy
who came from France.
He wore silk shirts
and purple pants.
And if you gave him
just a glance,
He'd jump right up
and start to dance.

18
am, clam, cram, dam, gram, ham, jam, lamb, ma'am, ram, scram, slam, swam, tram, wham, yam

19
aim, blame, came, claim, dame, fame, flame, frame, game, lame, name, same, shame, tame

20
camp, champ, clamp, cramp, damp, lamp, ramp, stamp, tramp

21
bran, can, clan, fan, man, pan, plan, ran, scan, tan, than, van

22
chance, chants, dance, France, glance, grants, lance, pants, plants, prance, rants, slants, stance, trance

23
and, band, bland, brand, canned, fanned, gland, grand, hand, land, planned, sand, stand, tanned

16
bald, bawled, brawled, called, crawled, drawled, hauled, scald, scrawled, sprawled, stalled

17
fault, halt, malt, salt, vault

24
bang, clang, fang, gang, hang, rang, sang, slang

25
bank, blank, clank, crank, drank, frank, plank, prank, rank, sank, shrank, spank, stank, swank, tank, thank, yank

26
ant, aunt, can't, chant, grant, pant, plant, rant, scant, slant

27
cap, chap, clap, flap, gap, lap, map, nap, rap, sap, scrap, slap, snap, strap, tap, trap, wrap, yap, zap

28
ape, cape, drape, grape, scrape, shape, tape

29
are, bar, car, far, jar, scar, star, tar

30
barred, card, guard, hard, scarred, starred, yard

31
air, bare, bear, blare, care, chair, dare, fair, fare, flair, flare, glare, hair, hare, heir, lair, mare, pair, pare, pear, rare, scare, share, snare, spare, square, stair, stare, swear, tear, their, there, they're, ware, wear, where

32
barge, charge, large, sarge

● ●

Two bears
Stood on the stairs.
I glared.
They weren't scared.

● ●

"Who's under that mask?"
I started to ask.
Finding it out
Was quite a big task.

33
ark, bark, dark, hark, lark,
mark, park, shark, spark, stark

34
arm, charm, farm, harm

35
art, cart, chart, dart, hart,
heart, part, smart, start, tart

36
ash, bash, cash, clash, crash,
dash, flash, gash, gnash, lash,
rash, smash, splash, trash

37
ask, mask, task

38
bass, brass, class, gas, glass,
grass, lass, mass, pass

39
blast, cast, fast, last, mast,
passed, past, vast

40
chased, faced, haste, laced,
paced, paste, placed, raced,
taste, traced, waist, waste

41
at, bat, brat, cat, chat, fat,
flat, gnat, hat, mat, pat, rat,
sat, spat, that, vat

42
batch, catch, hatch, latch,
match, patch, scratch, snatch

43
ate, crate, date, eight, fate,
freight, gate, great, hate, late,
mate, plate, rate, skate, slate,
state, straight, strait, wait, weight

44
bath, math, path

45
brave, cave, crave, gave,
grave, pave, rave, save, shave,
slave, they've, wave

18

46
awe, claw, draw, gnaw, jaw, law, paw, raw, saw, squaw, straw, thaw

47
all, ball, bawl, brawl, call, crawl, drawl, fall, hall, haul, mall, scrawl, shawl, small, sprawl, squall, stall, tall, wall

48
dawn, drawn, fawn, gone, lawn, on, swan, yawn

49
ax, backs, cracks, jacks, lacks, lax, packs, quacks, racks, sacks, shacks, smacks, snacks, stacks, tacks, tax, tracks, wax, whacks

50
bay, clay, day, gray, hay, may, May, pay, play, pray, prey, ray, say, slay, sleigh, spray, stay, stray, sway, they, tray, way, weigh

● ●

Wait, wait, till I open the gate,
Then you can skate. You can skate straight.
Don't skate till I open the gate;
Otherwise you won't be skating so great!

51

blaze, days, daze, gaze, glaze,
graze, haze, maize, maze,
pays, phase, phrase, plays,
praise, prays, preys, raise, rays,
slays, sleighs, sprays, stays,
strays, sways, weighs

52

beach, beech, bleach, each,
peach, preach, reach, screech,
speech, teach

53

beak, cheek, creak, creek,
freak, Greek, leak, leek, meek,
peak, peek, seek, sheik, shriek,
sleek, sneak, speak, squeak,
streak, tweak, weak, week

54

deal, eel, feel, heal, heel, he'll,
keel, kneel, meal, peal, peel, real,
reel, seal, she'll, squeal, steal,
steel, veal, we'll, wheel, zeal

Lazy days:
Sun's rays,
Blinding blaze,
Tree sways,
Cows graze,
Warm haze,
Lazy days.

55
beam, cream, dream, gleam, scheme, scream, seam, seem, steam, stream, team, theme

56
bean, clean, dean, green, keen, lean, mean, queen, scene, screen, seen, sheen, teen

57
beard, cheered, cleared, feared, neared, smeared, sneered, steered, weird

58
cease, crease, fleece, geese, grease, Greece, lease, niece, peace, piece

59
breeze, cheese, ease, fleas, flees, frees, freeze, he's, keys, knees, peas, please, seas, sees, seize, she's, skis, sneeze, squeeze, tease, these, trees, wheeze

60
beast, creased, east, feast, greased, leased, least, priest, yeast

61
beat, beet, bleat, cheat, eat, feat, feet, fleet, greet, heat, meat, meet, neat, seat, sheet, sleet, street, suite, sweet, treat, wheat

• •

Try not to sneeze when she's up on her skis.
The moment she feels the breeze from your sneeze,
She's liable to bump both her knees on the trees!
So please give your nose just a nice, tweaky squeeze,
And sneeze in the house where your nose cannot freeze!
Thank you.

• •

62
eve, grieve, leave, sleeve,
weave, we've

63
check, deck, fleck, heck,
neck, peck, speck, trek, wreck

64
bed, bled, bread, dead, dread,
fed, fled, head, lead, led, pled,
read, red, said, shed, shred,
sled, sped, spread, thread, wed

65
be, bee, fee, flea, flee, free,
gee, glee, he, key, knee, me,
pea, plea, sea, see, she, ski,
spree, tea, three, tree, we, wee

66
bead, bleed, deed, feed,
freed, greed, he'd, knead,
lead, need, plead, read, reed,
seed, she'd, skied, speed,
tweed, we'd, weed

67
cheap, cheep, creep, deep,
heap, jeep, keep, leap, peep,
sheep, sleep, steep, sweep,
weep

68
cheer, clear, dear, deer, ear,
fear, gear, hear, here, jeer,
near, pier, queer, rear, sneer,
spear, sphere, steer, tear,
year

● ●

If you stay at home in bed,
You will never bump your head
On a pole or sign or tree.
It's safe to stay in bed, you see.

● ●

69
cleft, left, theft

70
beg, egg, keg, leg, peg

71
bell, cell, dell, dwell, fell, sell, shell, smell, spell, swell, tell, well, yell

72
elf, self, shelf

● ● ● ● ● ● ● ● ● ● ● ● ● ● ● ● ●

*On a shelf
by himself
sat an elf.*

73
belt, dealt, dwelt, felt, knelt, melt

74
gem, hem, stem, them

75
den, glen, hen, men, pen, ten, then, when, wren

76
cents, dents, fence, rents, scents, sense, tense, tents, vents

77
bend, blend, end, friend, lend, mend, send, spend, tend

78
bent, cent, dent, gent, lent, meant, rent, scent, sent, spent, tent, vent, went

79
pep, prep, step

80
blur, burr, fir, fur, her, purr, sir, slur, spur, stir, were, whir

81
blurb, curb, herb, verb

82
curse, hearse, nurse, purse, verse, worse

● ● ● ● ● ● ● ● ● ● ● ● ● ● ● ●

83
blurt, dirt, flirt, hurt, shirt, skirt, spurt, squirt

84
curve, nerve, serve, swerve, verve

85
bless, chess, dress, guess, less, mess, press, stress, yes

86
best, blessed, blest, chest, crest, dressed, guessed, guest, jest, messed, nest, pest, pressed, quest, rest, test, vest, west, zest

87
bet, debt, fret, get, jet, let, met, net, pet, set, sweat, threat, vet, wet, yet

• •

Katie Baytee had a curse:
She only spoke in rhymes and verse.
Her mother took her to a nurse,
But after that, her verse got worse.

Boo hoo.
The bluebird flew.
Up the flue it flew, it's true.
Then it flew right out of view.
That's what bluebirds do to you,
They make you blue.
But then—who knew?

88
etch, fetch, sketch, stretch,
wretch

89
blew, blue, boo, brew, chew,
clue, coo, crew, cue, dew, do,
drew, due, few, flew, flu, flue,
glue, goo, grew, knew, moo,
new, shoe, stew, threw,
through, to, too, true, two,
view, who, woo, you, zoo

90
bib, crib, fib, rib

91
dice, ice, lice, mice, nice,
price, rice, slice, spice, splice,
twice

92
brick, chick, click, flick,
kick, lick, nick, pick, quick,
sick, stick, thick, tick, trick

In the jungle, Clyde the guide
Spied a tiger near the bride.
"Run and hide!" cried our guy Clyde,
But the tiger ate the bride.
"Well, I tried," sighed Clyde the guide.

93
did, hid, kid, lid, rid, skid, slid, squid

94
bride, cried, died, dried, dyed, fried, glide, guide, hide, lied, pride, pried, ride, side, sighed, slide, spied, tide, tied, tried, wide

95
beef, brief, chief, leaf, reef, thief

96
cliff, if, sniff, stiff, whiff

97
knife, life, wife

98
drift, gift, lift, shift, sniffed, swift, thrift, whiffed

99
big, dig, fig, jig, pig, rig, sprig, twig

100
bike, dike, hike, like, pike, spike

101
child, filed, mild, piled,
smiled, wild

• • • • • • • • • • • • • •

Once in a while
I'll walk a mile
To see you smile.

• • • • • • • • • • • • • •

102
aisle, file, I'll, isle, mile, pile,
smile, tile, vile, while

103
milk, silk

104
bill, chill, dill, fill, gill, grill,
hill, ill, kill, mill, pill, quill,
sill, skill, spill, still, thrill, til,
till, will

105
built, gilt, guilt, hilt, jiit, kilt,
quilt, spilt, stilt, tilt, wilt

106
brim, dim, grim, gym, him,
hymn, limb, rim, skim, slim,
swim, trim, vim, whim

107
chime, climb, crime, dime,
grime, I'm, lime, mime,
rhyme, slime, time

• •

Once I had a tiny chimp
Who had a gruesome grin.
And if you called my chimp a "shrimp,"
He'd kick you in the shin.

• •

108
blimp, chimp, imp, limp,
scrimp, shrimp, skimp

109
been, bin, chin, fin, grin, in,
inn, kin, pin, shin, sin, skin,
spin, thin, tin, twin, win

110
hints, mints, prince, prints,
rinse, since, splints, sprints,
squints, tints, wince

111
cinch, clinch, finch, flinch,
inch, pinch

112
bind, blind, dined, find,
fined, grind, kind, lined,
mind, mined, pined, shined,
signed, whined, wind

113
dine, fine, line, mine, nine,
pine, shine, shrine, sign, spine,
swine, twine, vine, whine,
wine

114
bring, cling, ding, fling, king,
ring, sing, sling, spring, sting,
string, swing, thing, ting,
wing, wring

• •

My uncle once gave me a strange-looking ring,
Tied up with paper and striped, straggly string.
Pushing the spring made the ring start to sing.
I wonder what next time my uncle will bring.

• •

115
blink, brink, chink, clink,
drink, ink, kink, link, mink,
pink, rink, shrink, sink, slink,
stink, think, wink, zinc

116
glint, hint, lint, mint, print,
splint, sprint, squint, tint

117
chip, clip, dip, drip, flip, grip,
hip, lip, rip, ship, sip, skip,
slip, snip, strip, tip, trip,
whip, zip

118
gripe, pipe, ripe, stripe, swipe,
type, wipe

119
brier, buyer, choir, fire, flyer,
friar, hire, liar, lyre, mire,
plier, sire, tire, wire

120
firm, germ, squirm, term,
worm

121
berth, birth, earth, mirth,
worth

122
dish, fish, squish, swish, wish

123
brisk, disk, frisk, risk, whisk

Does a worm
Make you squirm?

124
bliss, hiss, kiss, miss, Swiss, this

125
cyst, fist, hissed, kissed, list,
missed, mist, twist, wrist

Mama hen had twenty chicks;
Fourteen slept, but six did tricks,
Juggling bricks and dancing kicks,
And making monkeys out of sticks.

126
bit, fit, flit, grit, hit, it, kit, knit, lit, mitt, nit, pit, quit, sit, skit, slit, spit, split, wit

127
ditch, hitch, itch, pitch, rich, snitch, stitch, switch, twitch, which, witch

128
bite, bright, fight, flight, fright, height, kite, knight, light, might, mite, night, quite, right, sight, slight, spite, tight, white, write

129
myth, smith, with

130
give, live

131
dive, drive, five, hive, I've, live, strive

132
bricks, chicks, clicks, fix, flicks, kicks, licks, mix, nicks, picks, six, sticks, ticks, tricks

133
fizz, his, is, quiz, 'tis, whiz, wiz

134
buys, cries, dies, dries, dyes, eyes, flies, fries, guys, lies, pries, prize, rise, sighs, size, wise

135
boast, coast, ghost, host, most, post, roast, toast

136
blob, bob, cob, glob, job,
knob, lob, mob, nob, rob,
slob, snob, sob, throb

137
globe, lobe, probe, robe

138
block, chalk, chock, clock,cock,
crock, doc, dock, flock, knock,
lock, mock, rock, shock, smock,
sock, stock, tock (ticktock)

139
clod, cod, God, nod, odd,
plod, pod, prod, rod, wad

140
code, flowed, glowed, load,
owed, road, rode, rowed,
sewed, showed, snowed,
stowed, toad, towed

141
dodge, lodge, podge
(hodgepodge)

142
bog, clog, dog, fog, frog,
hog, jog, log

143
boil, broil, coil, foil, oil, soil,
spoil, toil

144
coin, join

145
joint, point

146
boys, joys, noise, toys

147
broke, choke, cloak, Coke,
croak, folk, joke, oak, poke,
soak, spoke, stroke, woke,
yoke, yolk

● ● ● ● ● ● ● ● ● ● ● ● ● ● ● ●

*The yolk broke,
And that's no joke!*

● ● ● ● ● ● ● ● ● ● ● ● ● ● ● ●

148
bold, bowled, cold, fold,
gold, hold, mold, old, scold,
sold, told

149
bowl, coal, goal, hole, mole,
pole, poll, role, roll, scroll,
sole, soul, stole, stroll, toll,
troll, whole

150
bolt, colt, jolt, volt

151
bomb, prom

152
chrome, comb, dome, foam,
gnome, home, roam, Rome

153
blond, bond, fond, pond, wand

154
blown, bone, cone, flown,
groan, grown, known, loan,
lone, moan, own, phone, sewn,
shone, shown, sown, stone,
throne, thrown, tone, zone

155
gong, long, prong, song,
strong, thong, throng, tong,
wrong

156
could, good, hood, should,
stood, wood, would

157
goof, hoof, proof, roof,
spoof

158
book, brook, cook, crook,
hook, look, shook, took

My dear Joan,
how you have grown!
Your legs are now so long.
My dear Joan,
how time has flown.
It's you—or am I wrong?

159
cool, cruel, drool, fool, fuel,
mule, pool, rule, school,
spool, stool, tool, who'll,
you'll, yule

160
bloom, boom, broom, doom,
gloom, groom, loom, plume,
room, tomb, whom, womb

● ● ● ● ● ● ● ● ● ● ● ● ● ●

Oh, gloom. Oh, doom.
My mother's giving me the
*   broom,*
And telling me to sweep my
*   room.*

161
croon, dune, goon, June,
loon, moon, noon, prune,
soon, spoon, tune

162
coop, droop, goop, group,
hoop, loop, scoop, soup,
stoop, swoop, troop

163
goose, juice, loose, moose,
noose, spruce, truce, use, Zeus

164
boot, brute, chute, cute, flute,
fruit, hoot, loot, mute, newt,
root, route, shoot, suit, toot

165
foot, put, soot

166
groove, move, prove, who've,
you've

167
blues, boos, brews, bruise,
chews, choose, clues, coos,
crews, cruise, cues, dues, glues,
lose, moos, news, ooze, shoes,
snooze, stews, use, views,
who's, whose, woos, zoos

168
bop, chop, cop, crop, drop,
flop, hop, mop, plop, pop,
prop, shop, slop, stop, swap, top

● ● ● ● ● ● ● ● ● ● ● ● ● ●

Winter snows,
Gusty blows,
River froze,
Heavy clothes,
Woolen hose,
Snowball throws,
Runny nose,
Frozen toes,
Lamplight glows,
Winter snows.

169
cope, dope, grope, hope,
mope, nope, pope, rope,
slope, soap

170
board, bored, chord, cord,
lord, poured, roared, scored,
snored, soared, stored,
sword, toward

171
boar, bore, chore, core, corps,
door, floor, for, four, lore,
more, oar, or, ore, pore, pour,
roar, score, shore, snore, soar,
sore, store, swore, tore, war,
wore, yore

172
dorm, form, storm, swarm,
warm

173
born, corn, horn, morn,
mourn, scorn, sworn, thorn,
torn, warn, worn

174
coarse, course, force, hoarse,
horse, source

175
court, fort, port, quart,
short, snort, sort, sport, wart

176
close, dose, gross

177
blows, chose, close, clothes,
crows, does, doze, flows,
foes, froze, glows, goes,
hose, knows, mows, nose,
owes, pose, prose, rose,
rows, sews, shows, slows,
snows, sows, stows, those,
throws, toes, tows

178
boss, cross, gloss, loss, moss,
sauce, toss

179
cost, frost, lost

180
blot, clot, cot, dot, got, hot,
jot, knot, lot, not, plot, pot,
rot, shot, slot, spot, squat,
tot, trot, watt, yacht

181
blotch, botch, notch, splotch,
swatch, watch

182
boat, coat, float, goat, note,
oat, quote, throat, vote, wrote

183
broth, cloth, froth, moth

184
both, growth, oath

185
couch, crouch, grouch, ouch,
pouch, slouch

186
bowed, cloud, crowd, loud,
plowed, proud, vowed,
wowed

Once there was a seafaring goat
Who spent all his days and his nights on a boat.
Then the boat hit a tree
And he fell in the sea
And learned very fast
   that goats do not float.

187
bought, brought, caught, fought, ought, sought, taught, taut, thought

188
bounce, counts, mounts, ounce, pounce, trounce

189
bound, clowned, crowned, drowned, found, frowned, ground, hound, mound, pound, round, sound, wound

190
crooned, pruned, swooned, tuned, wound

191
flour, flower, hour, our, power, shower, sour, tower

192
blouse, house, louse, mouse, spouse

193
bout, doubt, drought, out, pout, scout, shout, snout, spout, sprout, stout, trout

194
dove, glove, love, of, shove

195
dove, drove, grove, stove, wove

Spouse Finds Mouse in House!

196
bough, bow, brow, chow, cow, how, now, plow, pow, sow, vow, wow

197
blow, bow, crow, doe, dough, flow, foe, glow, go, grow, hoe, know, low, mow, no, oh, owe, row, sew, show, slow, snow, so, sow, stow, throw, toe, tow, whoa, woe

198
foul, fowl, growl, howl, owl, prowl, scowl

199
brown, clown, crown, down, drown, frown, gown, noun, town

200
blocks, box, clocks, docks, flocks, fox, frocks, knocks, locks, lox, mocks, ox, pox, rocks, shocks, smocks, socks, sox, stocks

201
boy, joy, toy

202
club, cub, grub, rub, scrub, shrub, snub, stub, sub, tub

203
buck, chuck, cluck, duck, luck, pluck, puck, struck, stuck, suck, truck, tuck

204
blood, bud, cud, dud, flood, mud, spud, thud

"Oh, joy! Oh, joy!"
Cried the girl and the boy.
"Mama has bought us our favorite toy.
It isn't socks.
It isn't frocks.
It's a bulging box of building blocks!"

Huff huff,
You're not so tough;
You think you're such a scary stuff.
Huff huff,
You're not so rough;
You're just a big bamboozling bluff.
Huff huff,
You're not so gruff;
You're just a piece of flimsy fluff.

205
booed, brewed, brood,
chewed, cooed, crude, dude,
feud, food, mood, mooed,
rude, stewed, sued, viewed,
who'd, wooed, you'd

206
budge, drudge, fudge,
grudge, judge, nudge,
sludge, smudge, trudge

207
bluff, cuff, fluff, gruff, guff,
huff, muff, puff, rough, scuff,
stuff, tough

208
bug, chug, drug, dug, hug,
jug, lug, mug, plug, rug,
shrug, snug, thug, tug

209
bulk, hulk, skulk, sulk

210
dull, gull, hull, lull, skull

211
bull, full, pull, wool

212
chum, come, crumb, drum,
from, gum, hum, numb,
plum, slum, some, strum,
sum, swum, thumb

213
bump, chump, clump,
dump, grump, hump,
jump, lump, plump, pump,
slump, stump, thump,
ump

214
bun, done, fun, gun, none, nun, one, pun, run, shun, son, spun, stun, sun, ton, won

215
bunts, dunce, grunts, hunts, once, punts, stunts

216
brunch, bunch, crunch, hunch, lunch, munch, punch, scrunch

217
clung, flung, hung, lung, rung, slung, sprung, strung, stung, sung, swung, tongue, young

• •

Bananas growing by the bunch
In the morning sun;
Pick one, peel one, for your lunch,
And eat it in a bun.

• •

218
lunge, plunge, sponge

219
bunk, chunk, drunk, dunk,
flunk, hunk, junk, monk,
plunk, punk, shrunk, skunk,
spunk, stunk, sunk, trunk

220
blunt, bunt, front, grunt,
hunt, punt, stunt

221
cup, pup, up

222
birch, church, lurch, perch,
search

223
bird, blurred, heard, herd,
purred, slurred, spurred,
stirred, third, whirred, word

224
cure, lure, moor, poor, pure,
sure, tour, your, you're

225
clerk, jerk, lurk, shirk, smirk,
work

• •

*Under the bunk
was a skunk.
Wow, it stunk!*

• •

Said the bird up in the sky,
As he flew away up high,
"I don't know exactly why,
But I have to say good-bye."

226
curl, girl, hurl, pearl, swirl, twirl, whirl

227
burn, churn, earn, fern, learn, stern, turn, urn, yearn

228
burp, chirp

229
burst, cursed, first, nursed, thirst, worst

230
bus, cuss, fuss, muss, plus, us

231
blush, brush, crush, flush, gush, hush, mush, rush, shush, slush, thrush

232
bush, push

233
bussed, bust, crust, cussed, dust, fussed, gust, just, mussed, must, rust, thrust, trust

234
but, butt, cut, gut, hut, jut, mutt, nut, putt, rut, shut, strut, what

235
crutch, much, such, touch

236
buzz, does, fuzz

237
buy, by, bye, cry, die, dry, dye, eye, fly, fry, guy, hi, high, I, lie, lye, my, pie, pry, rye, shy, sigh, sky, sly, spry, spy, sty, thigh, tie, try, why, wry

Alphabetical List
of the Rhyming Words in This Book

Alphabetical List
of the Rhyming Words in This Book

• •

WORD	PAGE	GROUP	WORD	PAGE	GROUP
band	16	23	bear	17	31
bang	16	24	beard	21	57
bank	17	25	beast	21	60
bar	17	29	beat	21	61
bare	17	31	bed	22	64
barge	17	32	bee	22	65
bark	18	33	beech	20	52
barred	17	30	beef	26	95
base	14	3	been	28	109
bash	18	36	beet	21	61
bass *rhymes with face*	14	3	beg	23	70
bass *rhymes with class*	18	38	bell	23	71
bat	18	41	belt	23	73
batch	18	42	bend	23	77
bath	18	44	bent	23	78
bawl	19	47	berth	29	121
bawled	16	16	best	24	86
bay	19	50	bet	24	87
be	22	65	bib	25	90
beach	20	52	big	26	99
bead	22	66	bike	27	100
beak	20	53	bill	27	104
beam	21	55	bin	28	109
bean	21	56	bind	28	112

WORD	PAGE	GROUP	WORD	PAGE	GROUP
but	41	234	care	17	31
butt	41	234	cart	18	35
buy	41	237	case	14	3
buyer	29	119	cash	18	36
buys	30	134	cast	18	39
buzz	41	236	cat	18	41
by	41	237	catch	18	42
bye	41	237	caught	36	187
			cave	18	45
cab	14	2	cease	21	58
cage	15	11	cell	23	71
cake	15	15	cent	23	78
calf	15	8	cents	23	76
call	19	47	chain	15	13
called	16	16	chair	17	31
came	16	19	chalk	31	138
camp	16	20	champ	16	20
can	16	21	chance	16	22
cane	15	13	chant	17	26
canned	16	23	chants	16	22
can't	17	26	chap	17	27
cap	17	27	charge	17	32
cape	17	28	charm	18	34
car	17	29	chart	18	35
card	17	30	chase	14	3

WORD	PAGE	GROUP	WORD	PAGE	GROUP
crime	27	107	cue	25	89
croak	31	147	cues	33	167
crock	31	138	cuff	38	207
crook	32	158	cup	40	221
croon	33	161	curb	23	81
crooned	36	190	cure	40	224
crop	33	168	curl	41	226
cross	35	178	curse	23	82
crouch	35	185	cursed	41	229
crow	36	197	curve	24	84
crowd	35	186	cuss	41	230
crown	37	199	cussed	41	233
crowned	36	189	cut	41	234
crows	35	177	cute	33	164
crude	38	205	cyst	29	125
cruel	33	159			
cruise	33	167	dab	14	2
crumb	38	212	dad	14	6
crunch	39	216	dam	16	18
crush	41	231	dame	16	19
crust	41	233	damp	16	20
crutch	41	235	dance	16	22
cry	41	237	dare	17	31
cub	37	202	dark	18	33
cud	37	204	dart	18	35

D

WORD	PAGE	GROUP	WORD	PAGE	GROUP
force	34	174	frisk	29	123
form	34	172	frocks	37	200
fort	34	175	frog	31	142
fought	36	187	from	38	212
foul	37	198	front	40	220
found	36	189	frost	35	179
four	34	171	froth	35	183
fowl	37	198	frown	37	199
fox	37	200	frowned	36	189
frail	15	12	froze	35	177
frame	16	19	fruit	33	164
France	16	22	fry	41	237
frank	17	25	fudge	38	206
freak	20	53	fuel	33	159
free	22	65	full	38	211
freed	22	66	fun	39	214
frees	21	59	fur	23	80
freeze	21	59	fuss	41	230
freight	18	43	fussed	41	233
fret	24	87	fuzz	41	236
friar	29	119			
fried	26	94	gab	14	2
friend	23	77	gag	15	10
fries	30	134	gain	15	13
fright	30	128	gale	15	12

G

WORD	PAGE	GROUP	WORD	PAGE	GROUP
goat	35	182	grass	18	38
God	31	139	grave	18	45
goes	35	177	gray	19	50
gold	31	148	graze	20	51
gone	19	48	grease	21	58
gong	32	155	greased	21	60
goo	25	89	great	18	43
good	32	156	Greece	21	58
goof	32	157	greed	22	66
goon	33	161	Greek	20	53
goop	33	162	green	21	56
goose	33	163	greet	21	61
got	35	180	grew	25	89
gown	37	199	grieve	22	62
grab	14	2	grill	27	104
grace	14	3	grim	27	106
grade	14	7	grime	27	107
grail	15	12	grin	28	109
grain	15	13	grind	28	112
gram	16	18	grip	29	117
grand	16	23	gripe	29	118
grant	17	26	grit	30	126
grants	16	22	groan	32	154
grape	17	28	groom	33	160
graph	15	8	groove	33	166

H

WORD	PAGE	GROUP	WORD	PAGE	GROUP
haste	18	40	her	23	80
hat	18	41	herb	23	81
hatch	18	42	herd	40	223
hate	18	43	here	22	68
haul	19	47	he's	21	59
hauled	16	16	hi	41	237
hay	19	50	hid	26	93
haze	20	51	hide	26	94
he	22	65	high	41	237
head	22	64	hike	27	100
heal	20	54	hill	27	104
heap	22	67	hilt	27	105
hear	22	68	him	27	106
heard	40	223	hint	29	116
hearse	23	82	hints	28	110
heart	18	35	hip	29	117
heat	21	61	hire	29	119
heck	22	63	his	30	133
he'd	22	66	hiss	29	124
heel	20	54	hissed	29	125
height	30	128	hit	30	126
heir	17	31	hitch	30	127
he'll	20	54	hive	30	131
hem	23	74	hoarse	34	174
hen	23	75	hoe	36	197

WORD	PAGE	GROUP	WORD	PAGE	GROUP
kind	28	112	**lace**	14	3
king	28	114	laced	18	40
kink	29	115	**lack**	14	4
kiss	29	124	lacked	14	5
kissed	29	125	**lacks**	19	49
kit	30	126	lad	14	6
kite	30	128	**laid**	14	7
knack	14	4	lair	17	31
knead	22	66	**lake**	15	15
knee	22	65	lamb	16	18
kneel	20	54	**lame**	16	19
knees	21	59	lamp	16	20
knelt	23	73	**lance**	16	22
knew	25	89	land	16	23
knife	26	97	**lane**	15	13
knight	30	128	lap	17	27
knit	30	126	**large**	17	32
knob	31	136	lark	18	33
knock	31	138	**lash**	18	36
knocks	37	200	lass	18	38
knot	35	180	**last**	18	39
know	36	197	latch	18	42
known	32	154	**late**	18	43
knows	35	177	laugh	15	8
			laughed	15	9

lock malt

WORD	PAGE	GROUP	WORD	PAGE	GROUP
lock	31	138	lull	38	210
locks	37	200	lump	38	213
lodge	31	141	lunch	39	216
log	31	142	lung	39	217
lone	32	154	lunge	40	218
long	32	155	lurch	40	222
look	32	158	lure	40	224
loom	33	160	lurk	40	225
loon	33	161	lye	41	237
loop	33	162	lyre	29	119
loose	33	163			
loot	33	164			
lord	34	170	ma	14	1
lore	34	171	ma'am	16	18
lose	33	167	mad	14	6
loss	35	178	made	14	7
lost	35	179	maid	14	7
lot	35	180	mail	15	12
loud	35	186	main	15	13
louse	36	192	Maine	15	13
love	36	194	maize	20	51
low	36	197	make	15	15
lox	37	200	male	15	12
luck	37	203	mall	19	47
lug	38	208	malt	16	17

M

68

N

WORD	PAGE	GROUP	WORD	PAGE	GROUP
peal	20	54	piled	27	101
pear	17	31	pill	27	104
pearl	41	226	pin	28	109
peas	21	59	pinch	28	111
peck	22	63	pine	28	113
peek	20	53	pined	28	112
peel	20	54	pink	29	115
peep	22	67	pipe	29	118
peg	23	70	pit	30	126
pen	23	75	pitch	30	127
pep	23	79	place	14	3
perch	40	222	placed	18	40
pest	24	86	plaid	14	6
pet	24	87	plain	15	13
phase	20	51	plan	16	21
phone	32	154	plane	15	13
phrase	20	51	plank	17	25
pick	25	92	planned	16	23
picks	30	132	plant	17	26
pie	41	237	plants	16	22
piece	21	58	plate	18	43
pier	22	68	play	19	50
pig	26	99	plays	20	51
pike	27	100	plea	22	65
pile	27	102	plead	22	66

Q

WORD	PAGE	GROUP	WORD	PAGE	GROUP
sheen	21	56	shot	35	180
sheep	22	67	should	32	156
sheet	21	61	shout	36	193
sheik	20	53	shove	36	194
shelf	23	72	show	36	197
shell	23	71	showed	31	140
she'll	20	54	shower	36	191
she's	21	59	shown	32	154
shift	26	98	shows	35	177
shin	28	109	shrank	17	25
shine	28	113	shred	22	64
shined	28	112	shriek	20	53
ship	29	117	shrimp	28	108
shirk	40	225	shrine	28	113
shirt	24	83	shrink	29	115
shock	31	138	shrub	37	202
shocks	37	200	shrug	38	208
shoe	25	89	shrunk	40	219
shoes	33	167	shun	39	214
shone	32	154	shush	41	231
shook	32	158	shut	41	234
shoot	33	164	shy	41	237
shop	33	168	sick	25	92
shore	34	171	side	26	94
short	34	175	sigh	41	237

WORD	PAGE	GROUP	WORD	PAGE	GROUP
sighed	26	94	skin	28	109
sighs	30	134	skip	29	117
sight	30	128	skirt	24	83
sign	28	113	skis	21	59
signed	28	112	skit	30	126
silk	27	103	skulk	38	209
sill	27	104	skull	38	210
sin	28	109	skunk	40	219
since	28	110	sky	41	237
sing	28	114	slab	14	2
sink	29	115	slam	16	18
sip	29	117	slang	16	24
sir	23	80	slant	17	26
sire	29	119	slants	16	22
sit	30	126	slap	17	27
six	30	132	slate	18	43
size	30	134	slave	18	45
skate	18	43	slay	19	50
sketch	25	88	slays	20	51
ski	22	65	sled	22	64
skid	26	93	sleek	20	53
skied	22	66	sleep	22	67
skill	27	104	sleet	21	61
skim	27	106	sleeve	22	62
skimp	28	108	sleigh	19	50

WORD	PAGE	GROUP	WORD	PAGE	GROUP
sleighs	20	51	sly	41	237
slice	25	91	smack	14	4
slid	26	93	smacked	14	5
slide	26	94	smacks	19	49
slight	30	128	small	19	47
slim	27	106	smart	18	35
slime	27	107	smash	18	36
sling	28	114	smeared	21	57
slink	29	115	smell	23	71
slip	29	117	smile	27	102
slit	30	126	smiled	27	101
slob	31	136	smirk	40	225
slop	33	168	smith	30	129
slope	34	169	smock	31	138
slot	35	180	smocks	37	200
slouch	35	185	smudge	38	206
slow	36	197	snack	14	4
slows	35	177	snacked	14	5
sludge	38	206	snacks	19	49
slum	38	212	snag	15	10
slump	38	213	snail	15	12
slung	39	217	snake	15	15
slur	23	80	snap	17	27
slurred	40	223	snare	17	31
slush	41	231	snatch	18	42

WORD	PAGE	GROUP	WORD	PAGE	GROUP
stayed	14	7	stock	31	138
stays	20	51	stocks	37	200
steak	15	15	stole	31	149
steal	20	54	stone	32	154
steam	21	55	stood	32	156
steel	20	54	stool	33	159
steep	22	67	stoop	33	162
steer	22	68	stop	33	168
steered	21	57	store	34	171
stem	23	74	stored	34	170
step	23	79	storm	34	172
stern	41	227	stout	36	193
stew	25	89	stove	36	195
stewed	38	205	stow	36	197
stews	33	167	stowed	31	140
stick	25	92	stows	35	177
sticks	30	132	straight	18	43
stiff	26	96	strain	15	13
still	27	104	strait	18	43
stilt	27	105	strap	17	27
sting	28	114	straw	19	46
stink	29	115	stray	19	50
stir	23	80	strayed	14	7
stirred	40	223	strays	20	51
stitch	30	127	streak	20	53

WORD	PAGE	GROUP	WORD	PAGE	GROUP
stream	21	55	sub	37	202
street	21	61	such	41	235
stress	24	85	suck	37	203
stretch	25	88	sued	38	205
string	28	114	suit	33	164
strip	29	117	suite	21	61
stripe	29	118	sulk	38	209
strive	30	131	sum	38	212
stroke	31	147	sun	39	214
stroll	31	149	sung	39	217
strong	32	155	sunk	40	219
struck	37	203	sure	40	224
strum	38	212	swam	16	18
strung	39	217	swan	19	48
strut	41	234	swank	17	25
stub	37	202	swap	33	168
stuck	37	203	swarm	34	172
stuff	38	207	swatch	35	181
stump	38	213	sway	19	50
stun	39	214	swayed	14	7
stung	39	217	sways	20	51
stunk	40	219	swear	17	31
stunt	40	220	sweat	24	87
stunts	39	215	sweep	22	67
sty	41	237	sweet	21	61

T

WORD	PAGE	GROUP	WORD	PAGE	GROUP
tow	36	197	trek	22	63
toward	34	170	trick	25	92
towed	31	140	tricks	30	132
tower	36	191	tried	26	94
town	37	199	trim	27	106
tows	35	177	trip	29	117
toy	37	201	troll	31	149
toys	31	146	troop	33	162
trace	14	3	trot	35	180
traced	18	40	trounce	36	188
track	14	4	trout	36	193
tracked	14	5	truce	33	163
tracks	19	49	truck	37	203
trade	14	7	trudge	38	206
trail	15	12	true	25	89
train	15	13	trunk	40	219
tram	16	18	trust	41	233
tramp	16	20	try	41	237
trance	16	22	tub	37	202
trap	17	27	tuck	37	203
trash	18	36	tug	38	208
tray	19	50	tune	33	161
treat	21	61	tuned	36	190
tree	22	65	turn	41	227
trees	21	59	tweak	20	53

WORD	PAGE	GROUP	WORD	PAGE	GROUP
wail	15	12	week	20	53
waist	18	40	weep	22	67
wait	18	43	weigh	19	50
wake	15	15	weighed	14	7
wall	19	47	weighs	20	51
wand	32	153	weight	18	43
war	34	171	weird	21	57
ware	17	31	well	23	71
warm	34	172	we'll	20	54
warn	34	173	went	23	78
wart	34	175	were	23	80
waste	18	40	west	24	86
watch	35	181	wet	24	87
watt	35	180	we've	22	62
wave	18	45	whack	14	4
wax	19	49	whacked	14	5
way	19	50	whacks	19	49
we	22	65	whale	15	12
weak	20	53	wham	16	18
wear	17	31	what	41	234
weave	22	62	wheat	21	61
wed	22	64	wheel	20	54
we'd	22	66	wheeze	21	59
wee	22	65	when	23	75
weed	22	66	where	17	31

y

WORD   PAGE   GROUP